JE LONDON Dream
London, Jonathan, 1947-
Dream weaver

AKRON-SUMMIT COUNTY PUBLIC LIBRARY
JUL 2005
DISCARDED

P9-CJL-763

RICHFIELD BRANCH LIBRARY
330-659-4343

# Dream Weaver

Jonathan London

illustrated by Rocco Baviera

SILVER WHISTLE • HARCOURT, INC. • San Diego   New York   London

Text copyright © 1998 by Jonathan London

Illustrations copyright © 1998 by Rocco Baviera

All rights reserved. No part of this publication may be reproduced or transmitted in any form
or by any means, electronic or mechanical, including photocopy, recording, or any information
storage and retrieval system, without permission in writing from the publisher.

Requests for permission to make copies of any part of the work should be mailed to the following address:
Permissions Department, Harcourt, Inc., 6277 Sea Harbor Drive, Orlando, Florida 32887-6777.

Silver Whistle is a trademark of Harcourt, Inc., registered in
the United States of America and/or other jurisdictions.

Library of Congress Cataloging-in-Publication Data
London, Jonathan, 1947–
Dream Weaver/Jonathan London; illustrated by Rocco Baviera.—1st ed.
p.    cm.
"Silver Whistle."
Summary: While walking on a mountain path, a young boy discovers a yellow spider spinning her web
and as he quietly watches her, he sees the world from a different perspective.
[1. Spiders—Fiction.]  I. Baviera, Rocco, ill.  II. Title.
PZ7.L8432Dr  1998
[E]—dc20       95-22799
ISBN 0-15-200944-2

Printed in Singapore
F H J K I G

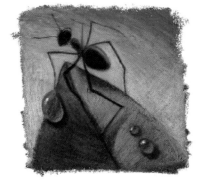

The illustrations in this book were done
using crayon pencil on recycled paper.
The display type was set in Jitterbug and Hollyweird.
The text type was set in Childs Play.
Color separations by United Graphic Pte Ltd, Singapore
Printed and bound by Tien Wah Press, Singapore
Production supervision by Stanley Redfern and Ginger Boyer
Designed by Lisa Peters and Rocco Baviera

For Norma Jacobson & Keene Saxon, with love

—J. L.


These drawings are in memory of my mother.

—R. B.

Nestled in the soft earth

beside the path,

you see a little yellow spider.

If you're quiet and listen,

maybe you can hear its feet

on the sparkling web.

Seeing you, Yellow Spider

seems to pause,

her legs like threads.

"Don't be afraid, little spider."

You smile.

Yellow Spider rests

and floats, silently.

So tiny,

yet the closer you look,

the bigger she gets.

A sudden wind,

and the trees hum,

the branches creak,

and Yellow Spider's web shimmers,

like wind across a pond.

But she hangs on

and you stay with her.

The whole world

is in these leaves.

Yellow Spider's world is yours. . . .

A raindrop on a fallen leaf is a forest pool.

An ant comes along. Stops. Touches the water.

Too deep. It backs up and circles around.

A tiny snail oozes along.

A giant! You watch, as still and silent

as Yellow Spider.

Then around a bend—crash, thrash, crash.

Too late.

When you look down

you find Yellow Spider on a leaf

beneath her broken web.

"There you are."

In the last light

you lift the leaf

and place Yellow Spider

near her tattered threads.

She waits,

then begins to weave.

Yellow Spider glows like the evening star,

gleaming over the sea

beside the crescent moon.

You want to stay

but it's time now.

Time to go home.

"Good-bye, friend. Good night!"

You run in the moonlight

down the mountain path

to your home in the valley.

That night in your room,

you climb into bed and close your eyes.


In your window

the evening star

hangs like Yellow Spider

on her invisible thread.

You drift into sleep and dream.

You are weaving a web,

flinging it out—

catching fallen stars. . .

then tossing them back to the night,

where they belong.

Good night.

Dream weaver.

# Some Facts about Spiders

1. Spiders have a lot of eyes. Many have 8 eyes
2. Spiders have eight legs. They are arachnids, not insects
3. Spiders can be as big as my hand or small like a dot.
4. Spiders live everywhere in the world. There's about 37,000 different kinds of them.
5. The yellow spider in this story is an orb weaver.
6. Spiders construct webs to catch insects. The insects get stuck in them. The spider then wraps them up in a blanket of silk to save for a meal later.
7. The stuff orb weavers and other spiders use to make webs is very strong. It's called silk and can be stronger than a steel string when made just as thick
8. If a spider weighed one ounce, it's web could hold four thousand ounces. So if I made a web it would hold 320,000 pounds. Even all my friends in school put together don't weigh that much
9. Spiders have been on earth for 300 million years.
10. Every night the orb weaver makes a new web It takes about one hour to make another one The orb weaver then eats its old web